To Bryton,
Have fun doing
your field work.

Gordon
1-25-12

If I Were a Farmer

a Farmer

Field Work

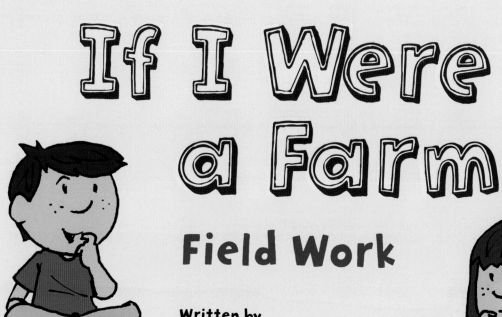

Written by
Gordon W. Fredrickson

Illustrated by
David Jewell

ISBN 10: 1-59298-340-5
ISBN 13: 978-1-59298-340-7

Library of Congress Control Number: 2010928524
Printed in the United States of America
First Printing: 2010
14 13 12 11 10   5 4 3 2 1

Book design by Ryan Scheife, Mayfly Design
(www.mayflydesign.net)

Beaver's Pond
PRESS

Beaver's Pond Press, Inc.
7104 Ohms Lane, Suite 101
Edina, MN 55439-2129
(952) 829-8818
www.BeaversPondPress.com

To order, visit www.BeaversPondBooks.com
or call (800) 901-3480. Reseller discounts available.

To my wife,
Nancy Ann (Simon) Fredrickson, with love,
for her wonderful work coloring and editing
the illustrations for *If I Were a Farmer: Field Work*
and for her tireless efforts doing real field work
and chores on our farm long ago.

Glossary

acre: an area of land measuring 43,560 square feet

antique: a very old object that may have value because it is beautiful, rare, or both. Farm equipment is usually considered antique after it is fifty years old.

auger: a shaft with a metal incline attached. When the shaft turns, the incline moves grain through a tube

blower: a large fan that sucks straw from inside a threshing machine, through a large tube, and onto a pile

bundle: many stalks of grain tied together with twine

cab: the sheltered part of a tractor or other machine where the driver sits and controls the machine

combine: a large moving machine that cuts grain and separates the grain from the straw

disk: a tractor tool with large, sharp steel disks that turn and break up the lumpy ground into smooth seed bed

dual wheels: when a farmer bolts a second wheel onto each single wheel of a tractor to keep it from getting stuck in the mud

field cultivator: a tractor tool that breaks up and mixes the ground in a field and then levels the soil to create a better seed bed

field work: any work done in the field to prepare the soil, plant the seed, or harvest the crop

four-wheel-drive tractor: any tractor that has power sent to all four wheels

grain: any of the grasses raised for their seed to feed humans and animals. Wheat, oats, barley, rice, and rye are grains.

grain binder: a device that cuts the grain, makes it into a bundle, and ties the bundle with twine

grain drill: a machine that uses disks to create shallow ditches in the soil and drops seeds into the ditches

harrow: a tractor tool with short steel teeth used to level the ground

hopper: a grain-storage tank on a combine

mustard: a hearty weed that can multiply and take over fields of grain

oats: seeds used for food for cattle and humans

plow: a farm tool with one or more heavy blades to break and turn the soil

seed bed: a place to plant seed; the surface of the field

shock: an orderly pile of six or eight bundles of grain, set on end in a field to dry and then covered by another bundle, which is known as the cap

spray: to cover an area with chemicals that will kill weeds or insects

straw: the dried stem of a plant after it has been separated from the seed

threshing machine: a machine that separates the grain seed from the straw

tile: sections of pipe buried in wet areas. They collect water and move it away from the field.

tractor: a vehicle with large wheels used by farmers to pull tractor tools called implements

wet spot: a low area in a field that remains wet when the rest of the field has dried out

Born in New Prague, Minnesota, Gordon W. Fredrickson was raised on a 120-acre dairy farm in hilly, rocky eastern Scott County, and like all the local farm children, he began farm work as a young child. Gordon served in the U. S. Army for three years, earned a Master of Education Degree at the University of Minnesota, and taught high school English for 16 years. During the first five years of teaching, he and his wife Nancy farmed 160 acres in western Minnesota where they raised cattle, hogs and grain. *If I Were a Farmer, Field Work* was inspired by that farming experience. Other books by Gordon include *If I Were a Farmer, Nancy's Adventure; A Farm Country Christmas Eve;* and *A Farm Country Halloween.* Visit www.gordonfredrickson.com for more information.

David H. Jewell was born in St. Paul, Minnesota, on November 13, 1974, and grew up in the rural town of Lakeland, located south of historic Stillwater, on the St. Croix River. After graduating from Stillwater High School, David attended the Columbus College of Art and Design in Columbus, Ohio, where he earned a Bachelor of Fine Arts degree. David presently lives in Minneapolis and works as a Graphic Designer and freelance illustrator. He enjoys spending time with his family, his friends and his service dog.